The Secret of the Lost Gold

Read more UNICORN DIARIES books!

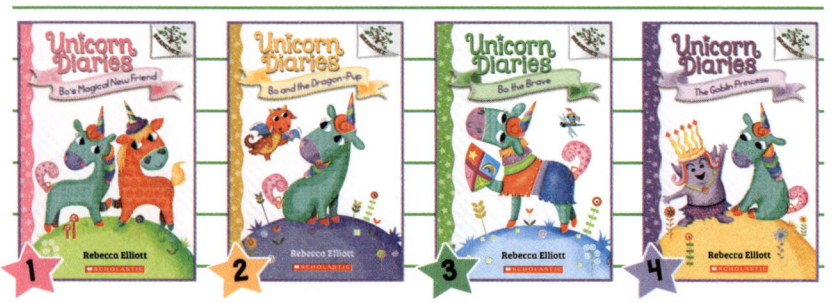

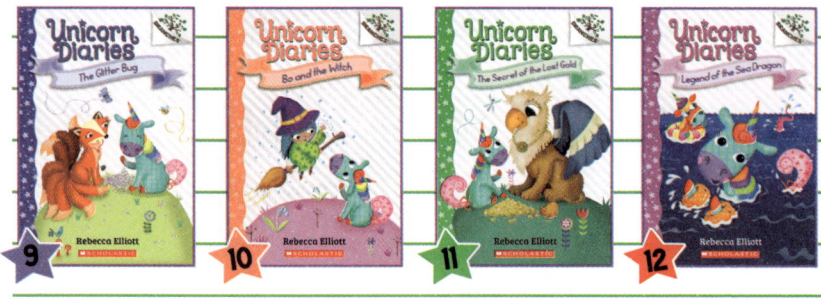

Unicorn Diaries

The Secret of the Lost Gold

Rebecca Elliott

SCHOLASTIC INC.

For Benjy and Toby, who have complained that I haven't dedicated a book to them in a while. Love you guys so much. XX — R.E.

Special thanks to Silje Watson and Diego Jimenez for their contributions to this book.

If you purchased this book without a cover, you should be aware that this book is stolen property. It was reported as "unsold and destroyed" to the publisher, and neither the author nor the publisher has received any payment for this "stripped book."

Copyright © 2025 by Rebecca Elliott

All rights reserved. Published by Scholastic Inc., *Publishers since 1920.* SCHOLASTIC, BRANCHES, and associated logos are trademarks and/or registered trademarks of Scholastic Inc.

The publisher does not have any control over and does not assume any responsibility for author or third-party websites or their content.

No part of this publication may be reproduced, stored in a retrieval system, or transmitted in any form or by any means, electronic, mechanical, photocopying, recording, or otherwise, or used to train any artificial intelligence technologies, without written permission of the publisher. For information regarding permission, write to Scholastic Inc., Attention: Permissions Department, 557 Broadway, New York, NY 10012.

This book is a work of fiction. Names, characters, places, and incidents are either the product of the author's imagination or are used fictitiously, and any resemblance to actual persons, living or dead, business establishments, events, or locales is entirely coincidental.

Library of Congress Cataloging-in-Publication Data

Names: Elliott, Rebecca, author, illustrator.
Title: The secret of the lost gold / Rebecca Elliott.
Description: First edition. | New York : Branches/Scholastic Inc., 2025. | Series: Unicorn diaries ; 11 | Audience: Ages 5-7. | Audience: Grades K-1. | Summary: In the dark woods, a griffin guards a secret cave and the old king's gold, but now Queen Juniper needs the gold to help restore the forest after a bad storm, so Bo and the unicorns seek out the griffin, hoping to explain their need.
Identifiers: LCCN 2024005138 (print) | ISBN 9781546127161 (paperback) | ISBN 9781546127178 (library binding)
Subjects: LCSH: Unicorns—Juvenile fiction. | Griffins—Juvenile fiction. | Magic—Juvenile fiction. | Severe storms—Juvenile fiction. | Diaries—Juvenile fiction. | CYAC: Unicorns—Fiction. | Griffins—Fiction. | Magic—Fiction. | Natural disasters—Fiction. | Diaries—Fiction. | LCGFT: Diary fiction.
Classification: LCC PZ7.E45812 Se 2025 (print) | DDC [E]—dc23
LC record available at https://lccn.loc.gov/2024005138

ISBN 978-1-5461-2717-8 (hardcover) / ISBN 978-1-5461-2716-1 (paperback)

10 9 8 7 6 5 4 3 2 1   25 26 27 28 29

Printed in India 197
First edition, February 2025
Illustrated by Rebecca Elliott

Edited by Cindy Kim
Book design by Marissa Asuncion

Table of Contents

1. Storm Watching — 1
2. The Big Storm Sleepover — 12
3. The Missing Gold — 20
4. The Dark Woods — 30
5. Edgar's Cave — 48
6. Fix the Forest — 54
7. A Golden Week — 66

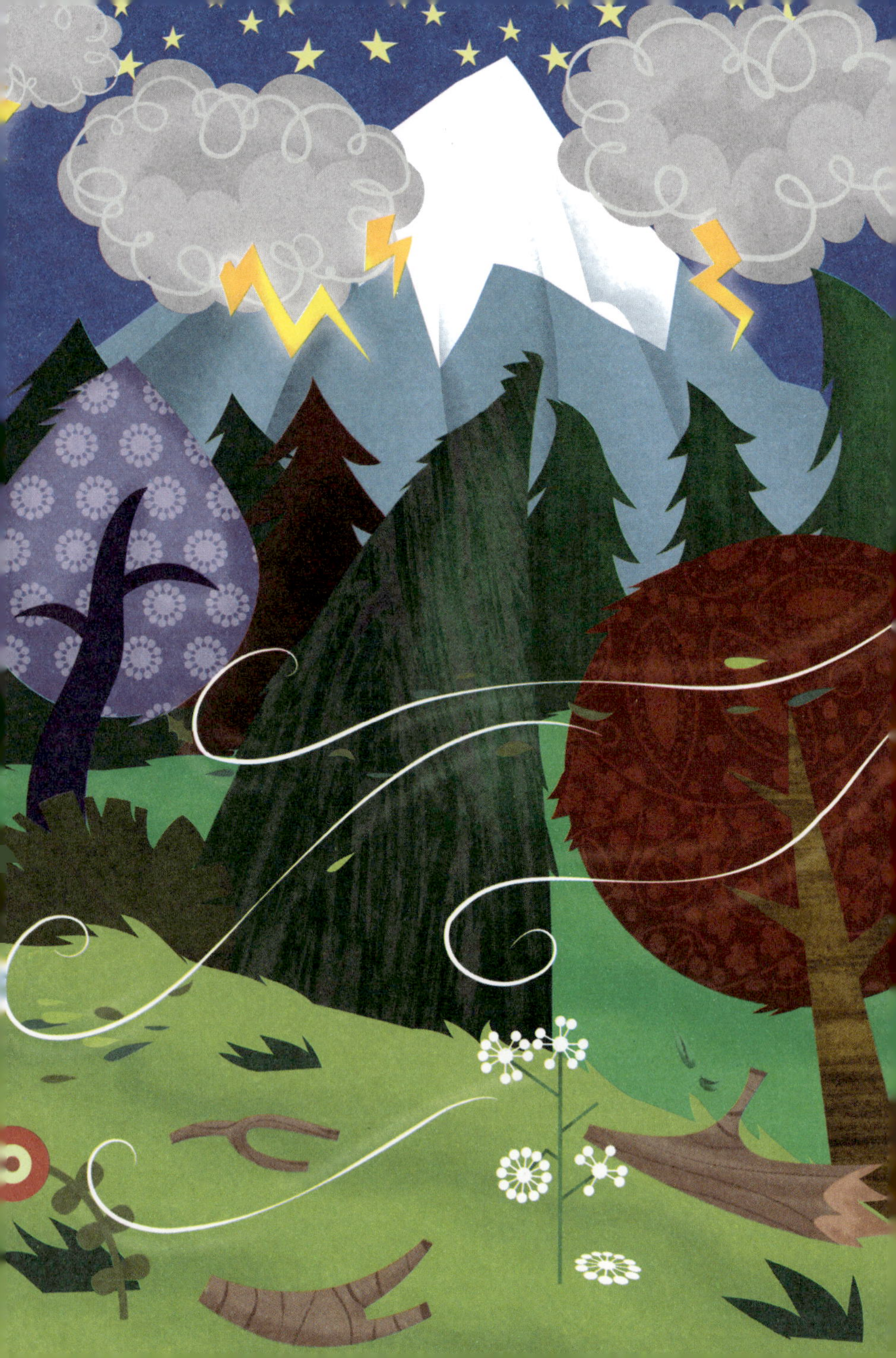

1
Storm Watching

Sunday

Dear Diary,
   SPARKLE-TASTIC greetings to you! It's me again – Rainbow Tinseltail! Call me Bo for short. Today I've been storm watching! The sky is filled with dark clouds, and lightning was spotted near Snowbelle Mountain.

This is a map of the **TWINKLE-TASTIC** place where I live.

It's called Sparklegrove Forest. Magical creatures of all sorts live here.

One of those magical creatures is the griffin. Griffins are fierce protectors and are really rare. Here are some fun facts about them:

They are half-eagle and half-lion. Griffins don't talk, but they do roar, squawk, and purr.

They can live for hundreds of years.

They live in caves deep in the Dark Woods.

They are very strong and brave.

Unicorns can be very brave, too. Here are some **GLITTERY-GOOD** facts about us:

Want to know a few more **UNIFACTS**?

We sleep on small flying clouds called **CLOUD BEDS**.

We love going on adventures. There are lots of areas we've never explored — like the Dark Woods.

Our bodies glow when we're nervous. The light from our horns also can be a handy flashlight.

Sparklegrove School for Unicorns (S.S.U.) is my school and my home! My friends and I live together in **UNIPODS**.

We all have different Unicorn Powers. I'm a Wish Unicorn. I can grant one wish every week.

My best friend, Sunny Huckleberry, is a Crystal-Clear Unicorn. He can turn invisible.

All my other unicorn friends have magical powers, too.

Nutmeg Silvertips 
Flying Unicorn

Scarlett Sugarlumps 
Thingamabob Unicorn

Jed Glitterock 
Weather Unicorn

Monty Dumpling 
Size-Changer Unicorn

Piper Forestine 
Healer Unicorn

Mr. Rumptwinkle 
our teacher
Shape-Shifter Unicorn

At S.S.U., we learn something different every week to earn a new patch. I wonder what patch we'll earn this week!

Mr. Rumptwinkle teaches us **GLITTERRIFIC** subjects like:

Unipod Building and Repair

Treasure Quests

Patchwork 101

Golden Glitter Fireworks

Wow, Diary! The thunder is so loud, our **UNIPOD** is shaking! I sure hope the storm doesn't come too close. Sleep tight!

2
The Big Storm Sleepover

Monday

Diary, guess what? The storm was really bad last night! This morning, there are tree branches on the ground everywhere!

Wow! I couldn't sleep at all last night.

I know, I was so nervous, I slept with one eye open!

Oh, me too. I barely got a wink of sleep!

The storm had been very loud, and it also left a very big mess all across the forest. We didn't know what to do. That's when Mr. Rumptwinkle joined us.

Last night's storm really stirred things up. There are many magical creatures who may be in trouble. Instead of having class today, we are going to see who needs our help.

Yes, that's a great idea!

So, we all split up and galloped to different areas of the forest.

The dragons' nests were broken, and fallen trees were blocking the entrances to the troll caves. Large branches were floating in Rainbow Falls, too!

But the great news was that no one was hurt.

We all brought some friends back to the **UNIPODS**. Sometimes, the best thing to do in times of trouble is make a pot of **PEPPERMINT-BERRY SPARKLE TEA**.

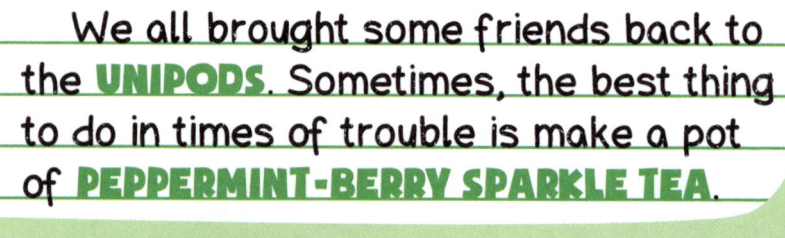

"Thank you, this hot tea is just what I needed!"

"Yum. These buttermoon biscuits are so tasty."

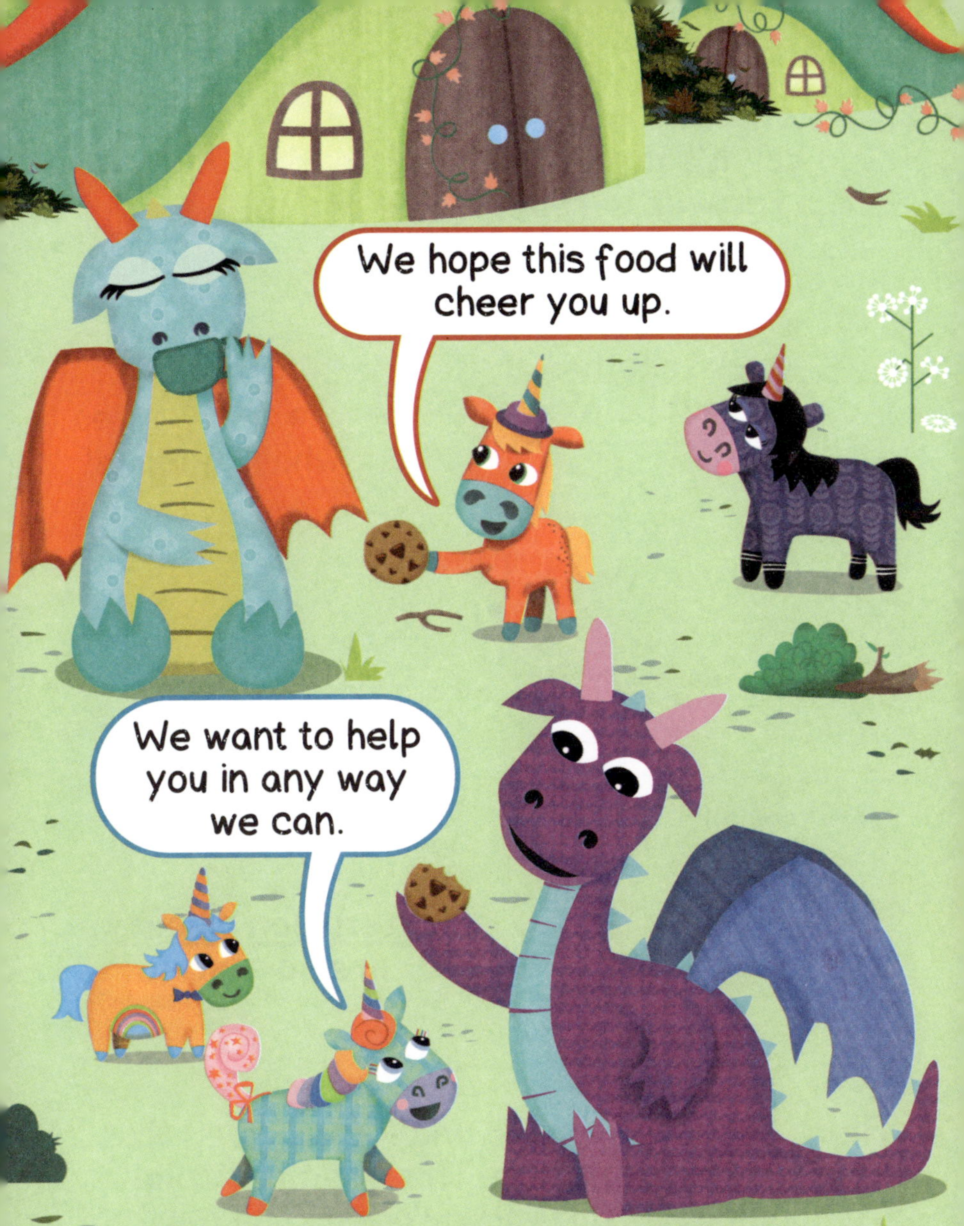
We hope this food will cheer you up.
We want to help you in any way we can.

After we ate and rested a while, it was time to figure out how to help.

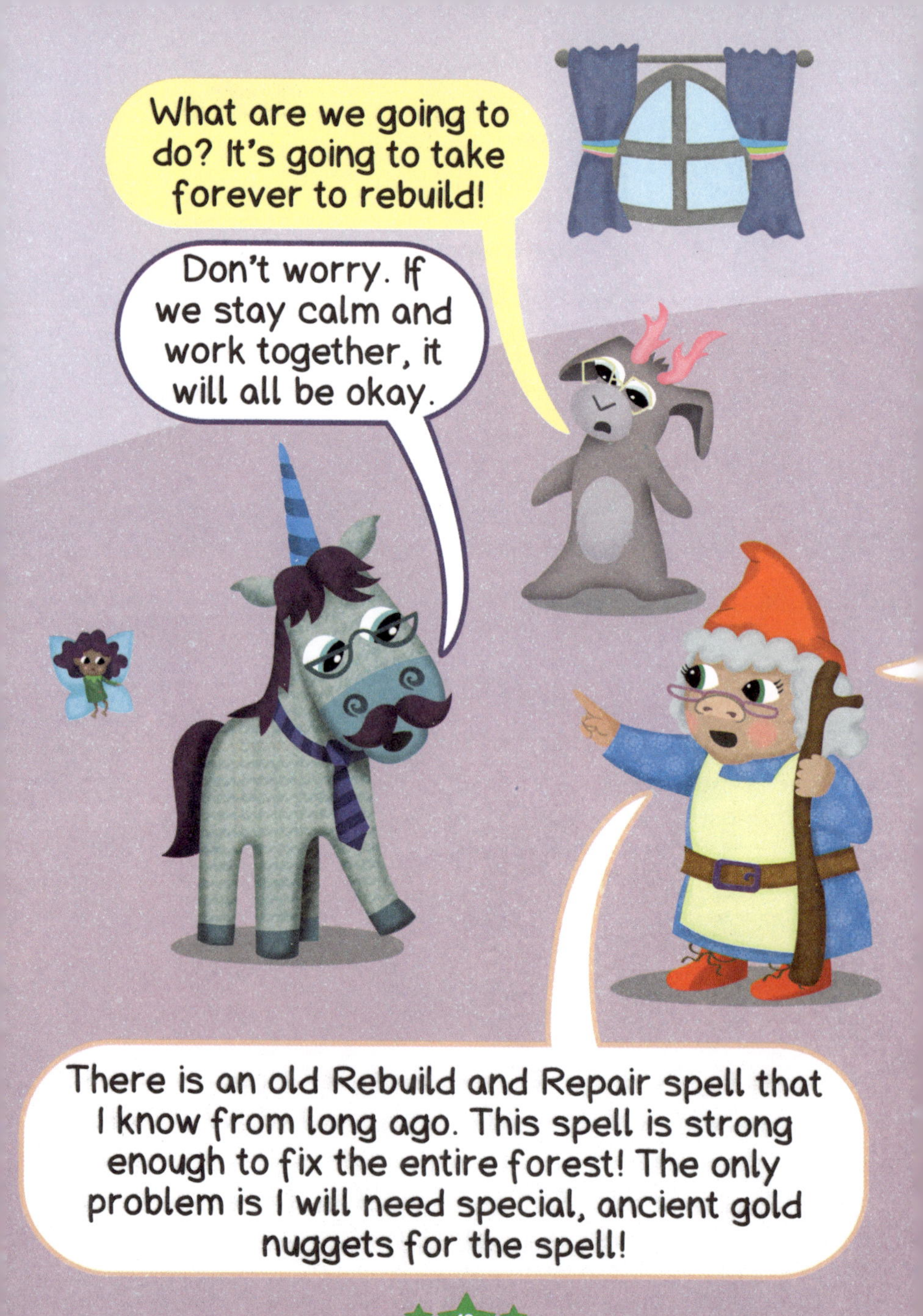
What are we going to do? It's going to take forever to rebuild!
Don't worry. If we stay calm and work together, it will all be okay.
There is an old Rebuild and Repair spell that I know from long ago. This spell is strong enough to fix the entire forest! The only problem is I will need special, ancient gold nuggets for the spell!

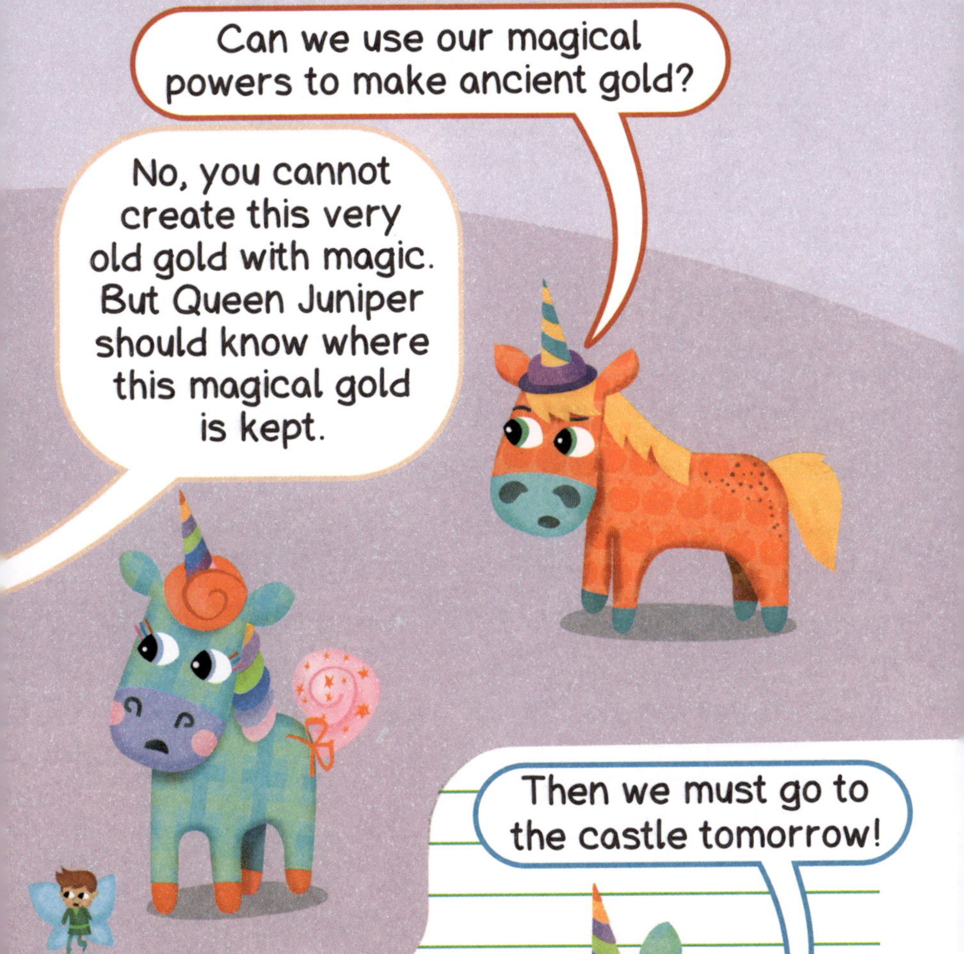
Can we use our magical powers to make ancient gold?
No, you cannot create this very old gold with magic. But Queen Juniper should know where this magical gold is kept.

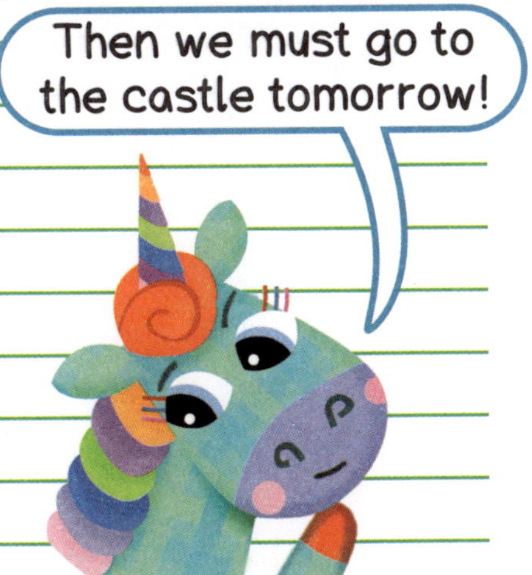
Then we must go to the castle tomorrow!

Oh Diary! I hope Queen Juniper will know where it is. Good night!

3 The Missing Gold

Tuesday

Today we arrived at the castle. The towers were still standing, good as new, but there was so much damage all around it!

"Oh no, look! There's such a big mess!"

"The castle gates are broken, too!"

"It looks worse than I imagined!"

As we looked around, Queen Juniper came over to greet us.

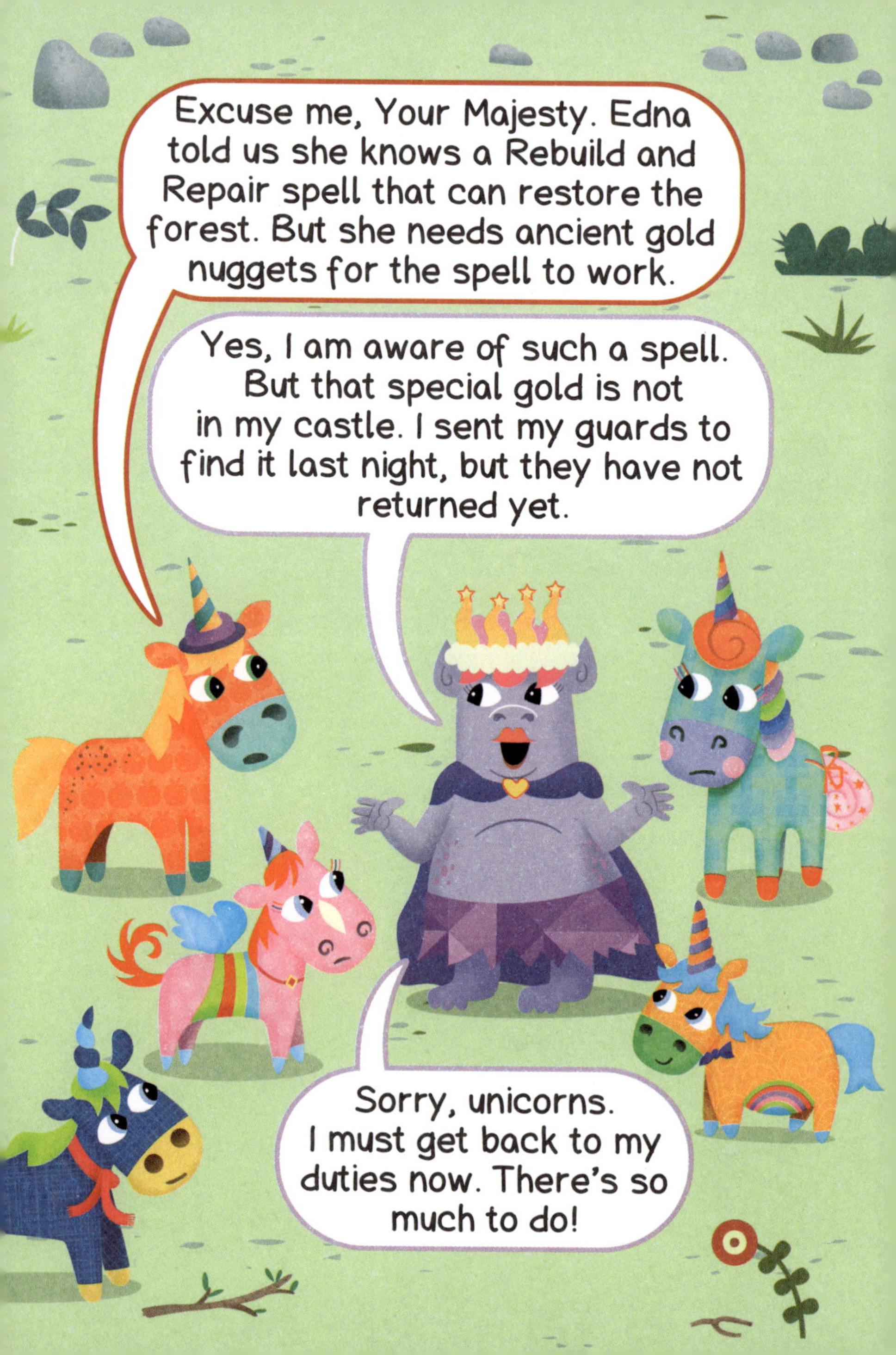

Excuse me, Your Majesty. Edna told us she knows a Rebuild and Repair spell that can restore the forest. But she needs ancient gold nuggets for the spell to work.
Yes, I am aware of such a spell. But that special gold is not in my castle. I sent my guards to find it last night, but they have not returned yet.
Sorry, unicorns. I must get back to my duties now. There's so much to do!

Most of our friends decided to head back to the **UNIPODS**. But Sunny, Nutmeg, and I stayed behind.

"It's a bit strange that the gold isn't kept in the castle."

"You're right! Maybe there's more to the story. Let's go and ask the princess!"

"Yes, Princess Greta knows all the royal secrets!"

We searched the castle grounds and eventually found Greta!

We told her we wanted to help rebuild the forest, but we needed to find where this ancient gold was kept.

I'm worried that this gold might never be found.

Why?

Well, because of the Secret of the Lost Gold. It's an ancient legend that my family has told for a very long time.

There's a legend? Like a famous story?

Yes! Do you want me to tell it to you?

So Princess Greta told us about the Secret of the Lost Gold.

A long, long time ago, the first king wanted the castle to last forever. So, he built it using special gold nuggets that held powerful magic. Then, he hid the gold in a secret cave. He was afraid it would get stolen and he knew that its powerful magic might be needed in the future.

We couldn't believe our ears!

But that's when a group of tired-looking castle guards walked by. So I had to ask for the scoop!

"Hello! Did you have any luck finding the gold?"

"No, something in the Dark Woods chased us away! It growled and stomped its feet."

"We're not going back there. It was much too scary!"

I saw Princess Greta perk up as the guards left.

"I know what scary creature the guards are talking about!"

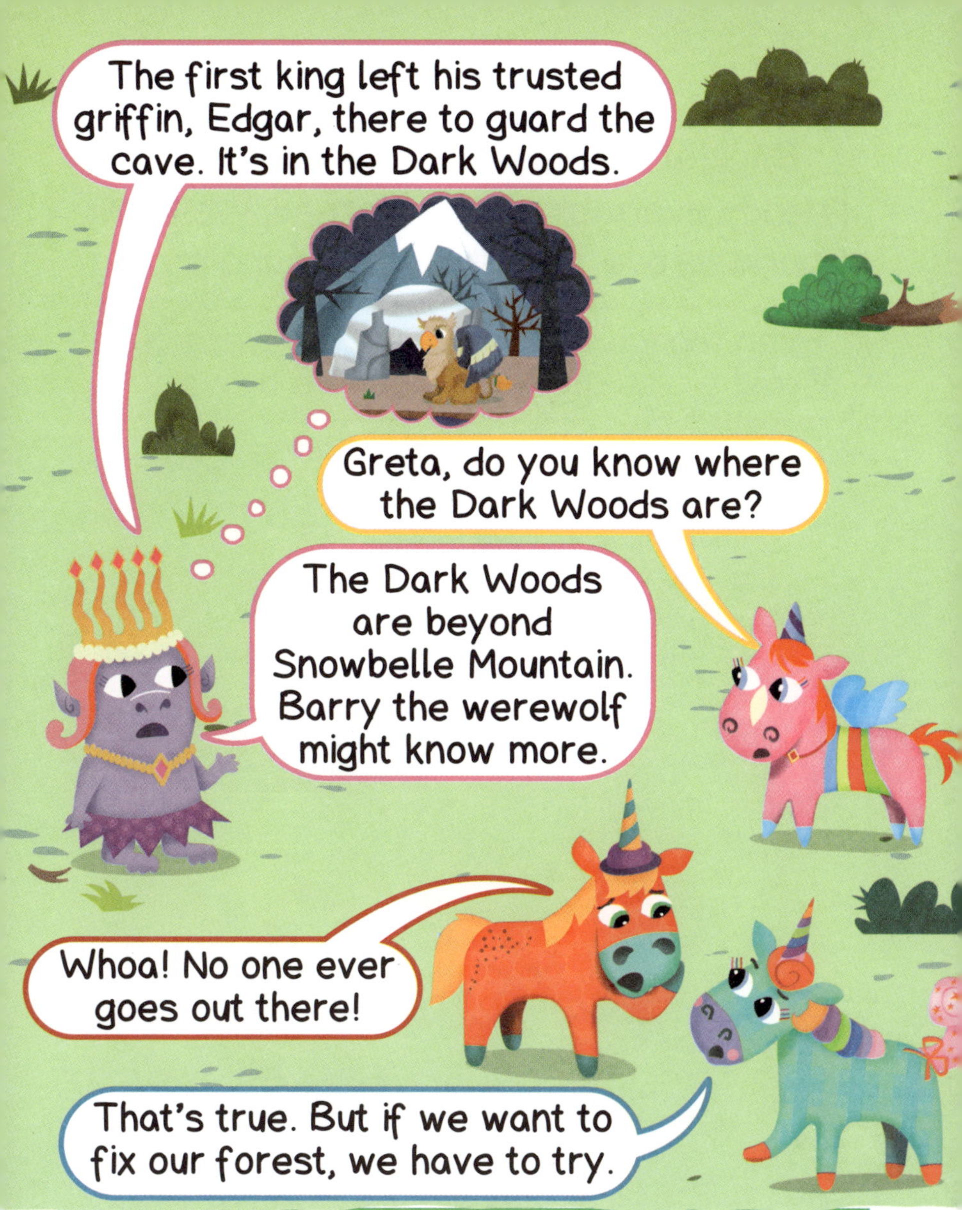
The first king left his trusted griffin, Edgar, there to guard the cave. It's in the Dark Woods.
Greta, do you know where the Dark Woods are?
The Dark Woods are beyond Snowbelle Mountain. Barry the werewolf might know more.
Whoa! No one ever goes out there!
That's true. But if we want to fix our forest, we have to try.

We thanked Greta for her help, then said good-bye.

Back at the **UNIPODS**, we told our friends everything we'd learned. We knew Sparklegrove Forest was counting on us.

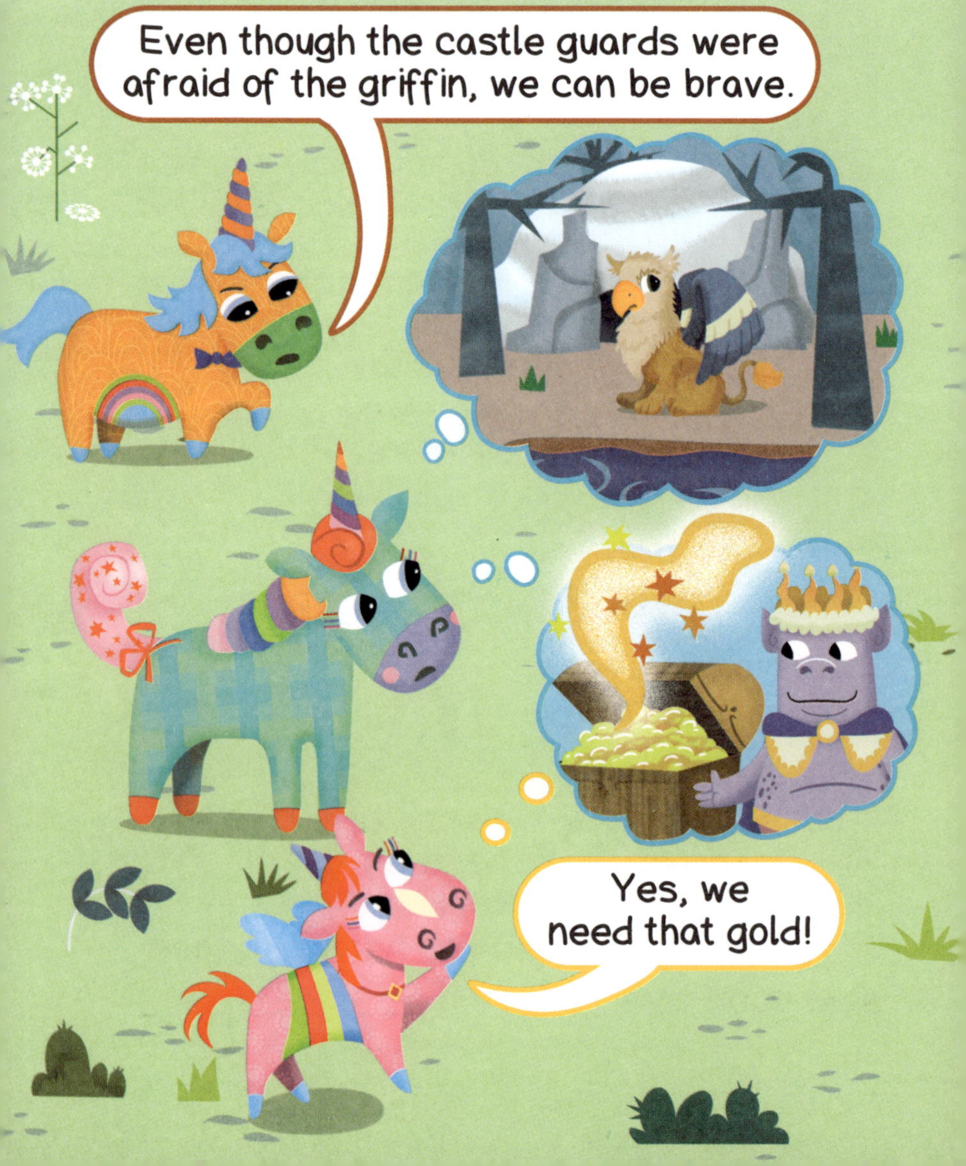
Even though the castle guards were afraid of the griffin, we can be brave.
Yes, we need that gold!

"I believe we can find the cave."

"I do, too!"

"Well then, our treasure quest will start bright and early tomorrow."

Oh Diary! I don't think I'll be able to sleep tonight. I'm way too excited to close my eyes —

4
The Dark Woods

Wednesday

This morning at breakfast, me and my unicorn friends got ready for our quest. We all thought the griffin wouldn't be happy with lots of visitors, so the seven of us set off on our own while Edna, Scorch, and our other friends stayed behind.

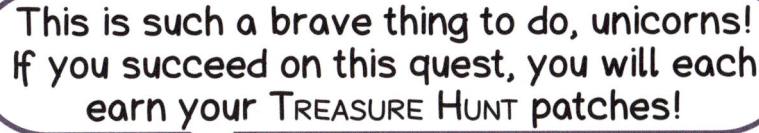

Then we set off to find our friend Barry the werewolf. We hoped he might be able to tell us more about the Dark Woods like Greta said.

We followed the sign pointing to Barry's Lair.

As we continued on the path, we saw a dark shadow approaching. So we hid behind the trees as fast as we could!

We were shaking in our hooves as we hid. Sunny even used his Unicorn Powers and turned invisible!

A few seconds later, a familiar voice called out to us.

We were so glad to see our friend.
Together, we happily headed inside.

Barry's Lair was very cozy. He made a pot of moon soup for us. Then we told him our plan.

Do you know where the secret cave of gold is?

The griffin has never been spotted. But I've heard rumors that he lives near Black Diamond Lake. That is the most dangerous part of the Dark Woods.

Oh no, it sounds like we're going to have a hard journey.

So we thanked Barry for the soup. He wished us good luck, and we said good-bye.

Soon, we arrived at the entrance to the Dark Woods. We used our horns to light the way. The storm had hit this area of the forest, too. There were tree branches all over the path.

Then, out of nowhere, a mean-looking giant came clomping down the trail. We all rushed to find a tree to hide behind. Luckily, giants don't have very good eyesight.

Monty acted fast! He used his Unicorn Power to make himself even bigger than the giant.

"You're not the biggest thing in here! I am! So please leave us alone!"

"How did you do that?! Oh fine, fair enough. You don't have to yell."

The giant walked away, and Monty came back down to normal size.

We all felt better as we continued on.

But that's when we heard a creepy noise. We looked around nervously. Luckily, we realized night sprites were making the noise.

Scarlett magicked up a fairy-sized radio and turned on a lullaby. Right away, the night sprites stopped fluttering.

"Look! Their tiny tree house is damaged!"

"That must be why they're upset. Let's help them!"

"That's a great idea!"

Piper quickly fixed their home, and the night sprites felt better. Then we all sang a cheerful song!

After saying good-bye to the night sprites, the woods somehow got even spookier. Suddenly, we were surrounded by grumpy talking trees! My hooves were shaking, but I tried to be brave.

How dare you wake me up!

There's no point in coming into these woods. You may as well turn back.

Look, we need to find something important.

And why are you so grumpy, anyway?

> No one has ever asked . . . but the tallest trees around here get all the rain first. So we are a bit thirsty.

> Oh! Well, I can help with that.

Jed swished his tail and some low rain clouds appeared. Gentle rain started to pour down.

The grumpy trees drank up every last drop of water. They slowly began to smile and stand taller. Just like that, they no longer looked spooky or grumpy!

The trees were so happy that they gave us shelter for the night.

Before bed, Sunny and I were talking about where to go tomorrow. The trees overheard us and gave us some advice.

Did you say you're looking for Black Diamond Lake? You'll find it if you keep going east. Just be respectful of the griffin who lives there.

Oh, thank you, trees!

Of course! Good night!

5
Edgar's Cave

Thursday

In the morning, we started trotting toward Black Diamond Lake.

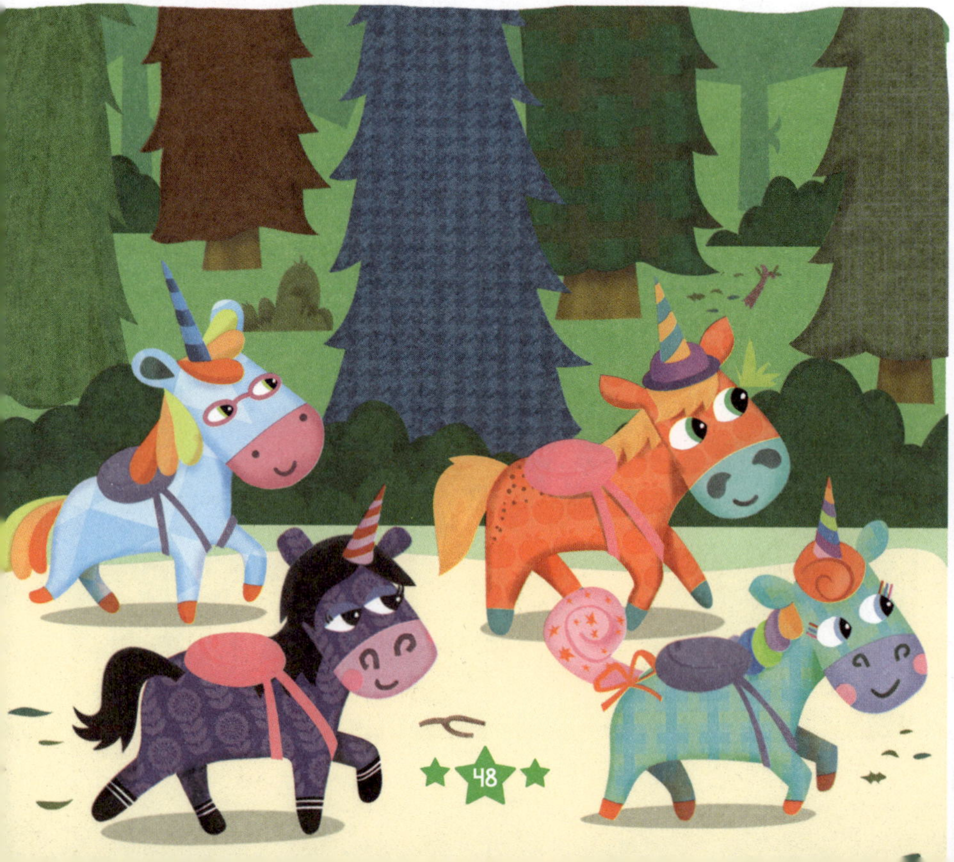

ROAR!

Then, Sunny found a trail of very large pawprints.

Sure enough, the trail led us to a cave where a fierce griffin stood! He wasn't happy to see us. At all. So we stepped back and waited. Then I took a deep breath.

> Hello, Edgar. We are unicorns who live in this forest. We need some gold from this cave.

> R-O-O-A-A-R-R!

> Oh no! RUN!

We ran behind the bushes. It was time to come up with a plan.

"Remember what Greta said — he's GUARDING the gold. He thinks we're here to steal the gold away!"

"He must have thought the guards were trying to steal the gold, too."

"Oh no, he's too upset to listen. I wish we could explain!"

"That's it, Piper! I have an idea."

I used my Unicorn Power to grant Piper's wish. Now the griffin would know that we only want to help!

This time, when I started talking, I knew Edgar understood we were there to help.

Edgar, we need your help to fix our forest.

Please, you can trust us to use the gold for good.

We waited patiently. Then Edgar let out a friendly squawk and let us into the cave.

Right away, a **TWINKLE-TASTIC** golden glow surrounded us.

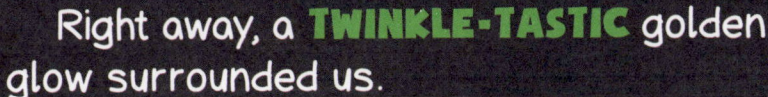

"Wow, look at all this gold!"

"Sparkling sunbeams! This will help everyone rebuild!"

"Edgar, thank you so much for keeping this treasure safe."

Edgar nodded as another adult griffin and a baby griffin showed up. Edgar had a family!

Thanks to our new friend, we were going to be able to restore our forest. But for tonight, we all cozied up together and fell asleep.

6

Fix the Forest

Friday

In the morning, Scarlett magicked up two sacks from her mane so that we could carry the gold.

That's when Edgar tapped his back with his tail.

"What is it?"

"Edgar is telling us we can ride on his back!"

"Oh, that's right! Griffins are very strong!"

"What a perfect plan! Thank you!"

Edgar nodded and knelt down. We tied the gold-filled sacks to his front legs and we climbed up on his back.

It was a tight squeeze. So, Monty used his powers to shrink down very, very small. Nutmeg could, luckily, fly beside us, too.

The trip back to the castle went much faster. We flew past the not-so-grumpy trees, who waved their branches.

Good luck, unicorns! Thank you for helping us!

As we neared the edge of the forest, we flew past Barry.

As we flew closer to the castle, our friends saw us and cheered. The queen's guards even blew their horns.

At the castle, Queen Juniper and Princess Greta welcomed us. Everyone jumped with joy.

Hooray!

You found the gold!

Yes! Edna can finally cast the Rebuild and Repair spell!

Edna dropped the gold nuggets into the cauldron to perform the special spell. The magic potion bubbled and sparkled.

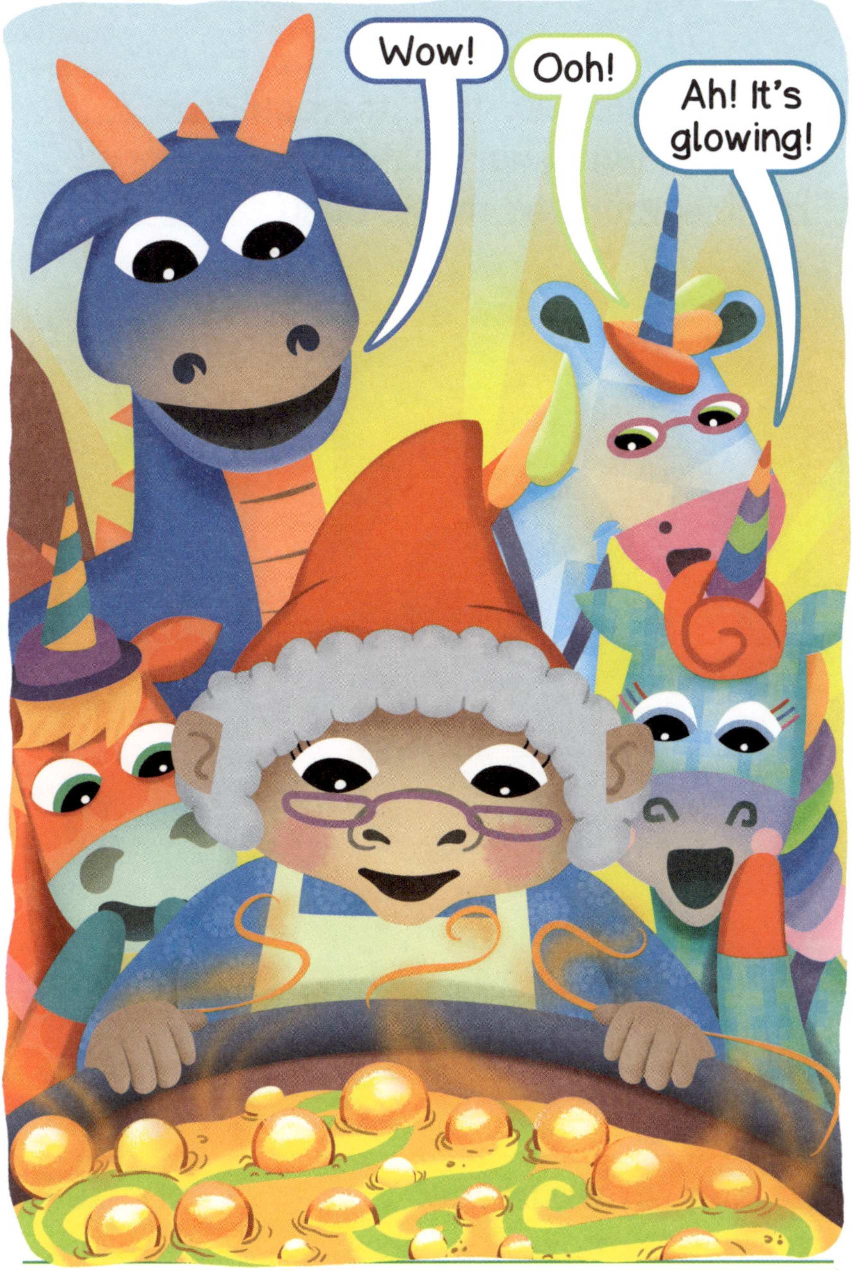
Wow!
Ooh!
Ah! It's glowing!

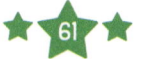

Then, just like that, the cauldron stopped bubbling. Inside, there was rainbow-colored magic dust!

Thank you for your help, Edna!

Now all we needed to do was sprinkle this dust across the forest.

We galloped over to the dragon nests first.

Wow! The magic dust is really working.

I can't believe it!

Thank you! My nest is better than it ever was!

Everyone worked together to rebuild our forest.

Edgar helped, too. Before we knew it, all our friends' homes looked as good as new.

As a reward for everyone's hard work, Queen Juniper decided to host a royal ball at the castle the next day.

"It will be the biggest celebration ever! Everyone in the land is welcome!"

"I'll have to polish up my hooves!"

"I can't wait!"

Lying in my **CLOUD BED** has never felt so good, Diary! Tonight feels extra special because our new friend, Edgar, is having a sleepover with us. We've all had a long day of hard work!

A Golden Week

Saturday

Wow, Diary! Queen Juniper's royal ball was **SPARKLE-TASTIC**! There was so much scrumptious food, lots of desserts, and golden glitter fireworks.

"Thank you, unicorns and Edna, for saving our forest!"

The queen awarded Edgar a majestic golden necklace as a special thank-you for protecting the forest's gold. Edgar gratefully bowed toward the queen, and I couldn't stop smiling. Griffins truly are very special creatures.

Then, Mr. Rumptwinkle gave us our TREASURE HUNT patches, and we all danced until we couldn't **TWINKLE TAP** anymore.

"Unicorns, you all did such a wonderful job! These TREASURE HUNT patches were so well-earned."

As the night ended, it was time to say good-bye to Edgar. We all gave him great big hugs. We were really going to miss our new friend, but he needed to go back to his family.

Thank you, Edgar. Please come visit anytime.

Edgar happily gave us a big hug. We had saved our forest together.

We knew he understood how thankful we were for his help. Edgar gave us a small bow.

I waved as Edgar soared off into the night sky.

Oh Diary, what an amazing week! We have a new friend in Edgar, and I can't wait to go visit the Dark Woods again. See you next time, Diary!

Rebecca Elliott may not have a magical horn or sneeze glitter, but she's still a lot like a unicorn. Rebecca always tries to have a positive attitude, she likes to laugh a lot, and she lives with some great creatures — her noisy-yet-charming children, her lovable but naughty dog, Frida, and a family of cats called Tomasina, Enzo, and Ferdy. She gets to write fun stories for a living, so she thinks her life is pretty magical!

Rebecca is the author of several picture books, the young adult novel PRETTY FUNNY FOR A GIRL, the bestselling Unicorn Diaries early chapter book series, and the bestselling Owl Diaries series.

Unicorn Diaries

How much do you know about The Secret of the Lost Gold?

What are five fun facts about griffins?

 Reread chapter 2. Edna tells the unicorns that there's a magic spell that can restore the forest. What is the spell called? What special item do they need to find?

In chapter 3, Bo and the unicorns hear about the Secret of the Lost Gold from Princess Greta. Write out the legend in your own words and draw a picture!

 Bo and the unicorns travel to the Dark Woods to find the griffin. What four magical creatures do Bo and the unicorns meet along the way? Reread chapter 4.

How does Bo use their unicorn powers to get Edgar to trust them? What was Edgar guarding? Reread pages 51–53.

scholastic.com/branches